I0606988

George Gerrard

The Consolation

George Gerrard

The Consolation

ISBN/EAN: 9783744714167

Printed in Europe, USA, Canada, Australia, Japan

Cover: Foto ©Andreas Hilbeck / pixelio.de

More available books at **www.hansebooks.com**

THE CONSOLATION.

A Poem.

BY

GEORGE GERRARD.

Toronto:

HUNTER, ROSE & COMPANY.

MDCCCLXXXI.

TO

W. W.;

OF THE MIDDLE TEMPLE,

This Poem

IS DEDICATED,

AS A TOKEN OF ESTEEM AND REGARD, AND AS A SLIGHT

APPRECIATION OF

HIS GENEROUS CHARACTER,

BY

THE AUTHOR.

PREFACE.

In presenting a volume for the consideration of the Public, it is usual to say something about it in a Preface, and I therefore take the opportunity to remark, that this Poem has been written with the endeavour, in all humility, of raising the thoughts and soothing the cares of man, as Keats hath it, however unworthy the attempt may appear. The noblest ideal that man can shadow forth to himself, must necessarily fall very far short of perfection, and the result, in seeking to attain it, will be even more imperfect, but the faculties that have been called into exercise, will receive increased power, and the time may come, when a first work shall acquire immortality from the value of the last.

GEORGE GERRARD.

Montreal, 1st December, 1880.

Tenor of the Argument.

I.

THE birth of Imagination took place with the expulsion of our first parents from Eden, who, on being driven forth to cultivate the world, were told that they should also people it.—Cain, therefore, was given from the Lord as a consolation, to turn their thoughts in a new direction.

II.

The anxiety felt by a mother for her first-born.—The hopes she images to herself of his future.—The mystery of possessing a living babe fills Imagination with delight.

III.

The season of youth, the spring-time of Imagination.—The deceit-ulness of the world soon robs youth of innocence.—Knowledge, the opposing weight to the world's attractions in the balance of human action.—Perfect Love and Friendship can alone give peace.

IV.

When middle life is attained, Memory increases the power of Im-agination, which becomes a greater consolation to the mind, enabl-ing it to indulge in noble trains of thought; such as arise, from contem-plations on the world, the birth and death of Christ, and the wonders of the Firmament. These lead to the consideration of Death, which

can alone be conquered by the means disclosed in revealed Religion,
which has used "the motions of Imagination as an instrument of
illumination," speaking to the mind by miracles and dreams.

V.

The further advance of middle-life, and correspondingly, early as-
sociations are dearer.—Imagination is strongest rising out of Memory
and Fancy, it animates and strengthens the mind.—The beauty of
Nature and the consideration of Beauty in the abstract.—The Lark.
—The consolations an antiquary finds in Imagination.—The slow advance of Progress.—Imagination the cause of Emigration from the
earliest times, as exemplified by the Greeks.—Athens.—England and
the Greek language.—The benefit of Contemplation.

VI.

Music.—It cultivates the emotions, generating sympathy.—It
soothes the mind, and fills man with Hope and Energy.—It is immortal.

VII.

Imagination can console the blind.—Literature a mainstay.

VIII.

Old Age.

"THE CONSOLATION."

I.

When man expelled by righteous Power,
From sinless Eden's love-built bower,
Felt mortal first, and knew Death's sting,
The wrath of God, high Heaven's King;
And from the Gates, a world beheld,
A lonely world, forthwith compelled,
In sweat of brow and aching back to till;
What thought alone that dreary hour could fill,
And half assuage a long reproachful grief,
And give the harassed heart some slight relief?
For joy and happy peace, could ne'er again,
Save mixed with sin and a proportioned pain,
His own through life, or hapless consort's be;
E'en now to guard Life's sacred tree,

High in the great archangel's hand,
A flaming sword waved o'er the land ;
It was the knowledge that a race should spring
From Love's embrace, and respite bring
To wandering thought, and farthest lands obey
The will of man, feel his enduring sway ;
That from the secrets of his partner's frame,
Would come a babe, when both might claim,
In contemplation of the newer life,
A brief immunity from ceaseless strife,
With that great Power, who o'er the soul,
By guileful force had won control,
And in the gift, sent from his home above,
Lose every ill amid a maze of love,
That home where first he drew life's breath,
Ethereal air, untainted by corroding Death—
Imagination, soothed his throbbing brow,
When pouring forth love's first deep vow,
Which since, a million tongues in every clime,
Throughout the cycles of departed Time,
Have uttered wildly in heart-thrilling tone,
Till clasped the arms each being they would own ;
Imagination was the fuel of his brain,

When first he gazed upon the infant Cain,
Nor thought, a brother's blood would lie,
And cause the man a wanderer to fly,
Upon those baby fingers then caressed,
And brand with murder's sign the form he pressed.
Round him, the first-born of the human race,
What proudest fancies could the father trace?
He knew no Paradise, no sweet abode,
Where highest love, in fullest glory, glowed;
But lived the Heir in undisputed sway,
To half a world, or where his feet might stray—
Disease and pain, with ills that now annoy
A transient life, and steal away each joy,
Were undeveloped through those earliest years;
Sin then, and its dim train of racking fears,
Had scarce marr'd man the image of his God,
With passions which do all the likeness rob;
Imagination wild, could in full freedom play,
And almost cause oblivion of the day,
When at the cool of eve that voice was heard,
Which broke the stillness and gave out the word,
Of changeless doom, unalterable fate,
And man forever passed through Eden's gate.

II.

When some fond mother sees upon her breast,
The first-born infant quietly at rest,
What happy thoughts fleet onward as she lies,
And oft escape half-formed, in gentle sighs ?
She thinks not of the past, for he has none,
On future years alone does sweetest fancy run,
And builds up castles for the darling's sake ;
How she will early teach him to partake,
Of the high functions of their native state,
Where history shall upon his footsteps wait,
And dark oppression in a distant land,
Shake and be quenched at dread of his demand ;
And lonely exiles languishing away,
Beyond the portals of the summer day,
For that great crime, of yearning to be free,
Their homes, their fireside homes will see !
A sudden tremor passes o'er her frame,
What! If my son the villains now could claim,
His youthful lot, the useless destiny of those,
Who rot and moulder 'mid Siberian snows,
Had he been born beneath the iron heels,

That tread on Liberty, where Despotism steals
The rising life from depths of ardent hearts,
And vilest tyranny and lust imparts—
Oh ! will he on the paths of learning stray,
And all false doubt by force of genius slay;
Will he shed lustre round about his clan,
And spring to fame, God-gifted as a man !
Or shall divinest music seize his soul,
In its mysterious grasp of limitless control,
Which over votaries commands such thrall,
That at its lowliest shrine enraptured fall,
The savage tribes of desert wastes,
When once each spirit, the delirium tastes !
Swift, in a sharp review before her mind,
Each art, each science places find,
All from a mother's standpoint is surveyed,
And reasons for, against, are duly weighed—
The mighty deeds of heroes long since dead,
Who for their hearths upon the battle-field had bled,
Whose soaring spirits joined the martyr throng,
Immortal then to live, in greater epic song,
Rise up and sweep in quick succession past;
A patriot's glory shall endure and last,

With human life, to end of latest time,
Buds forth on Earth to bloom in Heaven's clime;
This, this she knows, but O, the tender heart,
Shrinks from the shock of arms, for art
Has overturned war's ancient tactics now,
E'en the Black Brunswicker might vow   [none—
His ghastly oath—to take no quarter and give
A mile away, comes from the polished gun,
Death's leaden messenger upon the air,   [care?
Its objects strikes—who does for the poor victim
And as this thought Imagination brings,
In all its full reality, on rapid wings,
The thinking mother gives a sudden start,
And louder throbs the fond maternal heart;
When he, the placid slumberer on that breast,
Wakes from the warm invigorating rest,
Opes his small eyes of liquid blue,
In which already gleams the spirit through;
As may be seen when passion works behind,
In the ungrown, half-conscious mind.
The tiny hand feels for the bosom's food;
No timid stranger does it there intrude;
Its little fingers press the yielding form,

Which issues nourishment against life's storm,
And happy arms encircle him again,
Imagination running through the brain ;
And happy eyes that beam with happier smiles
Gaze long and lovingly upon the baby's wiles.

III.

Soon into youth,—how soon we grow !—
That time of pleasure's wildest flow,
For life looks brilliant, Hope runs high,
And points aspiring genius to the sky ;
Though older years evolve a different tale,
When every joy by foul disease must pale.
Could Youth, could happy youth immortal be
And bloom renewed as seasons flee,
What charms would then Imagination give,
When its first blush should ever live ?
As children, through a summer's day,
Chase busy butterflies in colours gay,
O'er fields where larks delighted sing,
While soaring high on joyous wing,
And pleasing landscapes shining bright,
Reflect again the glistening sunlight ;

So is imagination to the fervid mind,
A holiday to thought and youth combined ;
Not the dull sluggard who from even way,
Can ne'er to other pastimes, higher stray,
Is his the lot from self to be unfurled,
And revel in creations of another world.
The ills of life too many are, for one,
Unless this transient race is well-nigh run,
Long on the dark side of the earth to rest,
Know not the merry feast and be the welcome guest.
Yet I would not thus chide the heart,
When heavy sorrow anguish does impart,
For some dear friend, wrapped in the murky gloom,
The silent darkness of the fetid tomb ;
For him in truth the hum of active life,
Opes up each wound as with the sharpest knife,
Though here, Imagination pleasure gives,
And roams to regions where the Spirit lives ;
But one, who lost in lethargy, ne'er feels
The wild commotion, as the heart-blood steals,
Like Lava's tide, along each swelling vein,
Till all aglow it mounts into the brain,
Can never know the soul's exulting hour,

Born from that thought, the consciousness of power;
But he, the youth, whose ever glowing eyes,
Reflect an ardour full of enterprise ;
What joys are his, as up he quickly grows,
And deeper wonders education shows.
Life is too short, e'en now the dreaded end,
Already looms within the misty bend
Of future years, where turning round, he must
Descend again, down rapidly to dust;
But not discouraged is the ardent mind,
As ever onward, greater truths to find,
It presses with untiring strength and mighty soul,
And may at length come near the wished-for goal.
Life he enjoys, 'tis right we should enjoy,
The world around, free from the world's alloy;
And nature blooms for him in loveliest form,
Or louder rolls with threatening force the storm,
Till thoughts arise, that never quenched will be,
And give a longing other lands to see,
And if perchance sweet fortune is his lot,
The wide, wide earth, has not a blackened spot.
Oh youth ! How beautiful are thy young dreams,
How rich with pictures lively fancy teems,

B

How guileless thy too trusting breast,

What perfect faith the early years attest?

And must thy purity be thrown aside,

When worldly cares the bosom's cares divide;

And in Society's mad race for fame,

A glittering bauble scarcely worth the name,

The union point of coldness and deceit,

Where Self and Scandal, twin-like, meet,

With bitter feuds, with jealousies that tear ¦

The smile of innocence from what was fair,

Be lost the precious jewel of thy early life;

And plunged amid the sickening strife,

With sordid Sycophant, and Parasite,

Must with their worthless weapons fight,

Bow low the knee before the parvenu,

Feel all the loathing of his varied hue,

And rub thyself, in swine-like state,

Against the lowest pillars of his gate, *

In fear they leave you coldly and pass by,

To yon base worm, whose riches lie,

Producing nought, like weeds in garden bed,

---

* Socrates says in "The Memorabilia," "Critias seemed to him to have some feeling like that of a pig, as he wished to rub against Euthydemus, as swine against stones."

Till rose and thorn are almost wed,

For want of one to sweep the dirt away,

Ere fairest earth becomes contaminated clay.

No! rather no! Mix not with such as these,

Who use the arts to make them please,

When once is gathered all that can be got,

Soon thou wilt mourn thy foolish lot;

But stand serene, and from thy lofty place,

With calmest eye their wild gyrations trace,

How some will lower cringe than others can,

To win the smile of wealth's successful man,

Who once walked on the world unknown,

While all rush now a bosom friend to own.

Though thus, O youth; O lovely blooming youth,

Are tarnished thy bright dreams, when truth

Held chiefest sway upon the mind,

Ere loathsome contact every charm confined,

Not yet shall sweet Imagination cease,

To yield her full delights of tranquil peace;

Far from the giddy, brainless whirl of those,

Who do not breathe save where excitement grows,

Who know not pleasure in the only thing,

Which will to latest age contentment bring;

Deep in communion with thy better self,
Free from the worshippers of worthless pelf,
In fondest intercourse with sages gone,
Whose light ne'er waned, but brighter shone,
Whose genius lived, more glory gave,
And still illumes the silence of the grave,
Shall you receive a portion of that joy,
Which cannot fade, or truest nature cloy ;
Imagination tempered in affliction's fire,
Will lose its blush, but greater strength acquire,
And down amid the hidden springs of thought,
The spell shall rise; its potency, when sought,
Will soothe the world's asperities to sleep,
And sweet oblivion of the present keep.
If warmest passion o'er the bosom steals,
And Romeo before his Juliet kneels,
For Genius has love's ardour felt,
The man of learning unto Venus knelt ;
Or if the heart in friendship's firmest ties,
Holds happy intercourse and every change defies ;
If Intellect can bravely love an intellect,
And nothing mundane each infect,
Then out from Fancy's kingdom rolls,

The perfect union of two kindred souls.

When pulse and pulse together beat,

And thought and thought in rapture meet,

In fairest clime exists no higher bliss,

Save when the lips are pressed to kiss ;

And she first knows, upon that hour,

The strength of love's consuming power ;

How she must sink beneath its weight,

If half the joyousness, thrice happy fate,

Was not by him with equal ardour shared,

And heart to heart in purity is bared

Imagination, here unwillingly recoils,

For in Love's labyrinthine toils,

The wildest scope would not sufficient be,

To sing to mortal mind its immortality ;

Love knows no bounds, its spirit cannot die,

But freshly blossoms as the ages fly,

Forever blooming with the hue of youth,

Forever stronger nearest to the truth,

Throughout all Time, Love is the guiding star,

Which points us onward from its seat afar ;

Bids us rejoice, to live for life, for light again,

Where peace and happiness shall hold their reign ;

The most phlegmatic temperament burns,
A brighter flame, when love the heart once learns,
In firm dominion o'er the troubled breast,
The highest love, alone can promise rest ;
Will bear the soul in upward course away,
And mightier grow in Heaven's eternal day.

IV.

When youth's warm impulses have flown,
And half-way in the span of life alone,
We stand one moment 'mid the rolling years,
While the dim future through the age appears ;
As when one climbs to mountain height,
And pauses long with lingering sight,
To scan the wide horizon and the scene,
The lovely prospect's varying tints of green
Clad with the sunshine fading to the West
And nature calmly peaceful looks its best ;
Ere one must cross the rugged brow and find,
The shades of summer soon are left behind,
Which ne'er again the eager eyes will see,
But henceforth 'mid a dreary winter be ;
Fond memory will cluster round the days,

With beaming love in every backward gaze,
When earliest charms and sweet delights were known,
And friendships formed that could for grief atone ;
And imperceptibly man creeps to middle life,
Leaves far behind the faction burning strife,
Feels greater pleasure as Imagination holds,
The Goddess Memory in bands of silken folds,
When both are bound by closely knitted ties,
Which firmer grow as onward flies,
The time that leads towards Lethe's wave,
And wait the hands to bear him to the grave.
Full wisdom has matured the thinking mind,
Which to its destined lot is then resigned,
Ambitious youth no more upon it preys,
And hollow falls the flatterer's praise,
From dearest volumes is the knowledge won,
Round which all nations gather into one,
That tell how highest contemplations seek,
To fathom mysteries as Ocean deep.
What thoughts are greater, more sublime,
Than those that dwell on wonders of our clime,
Our mighty Earth, which holds its ordered place,
In the unlimitable breadth of space ;

As when amid the unknown ages past,
Its shapeless mass from wondrous mould was cast;
Its sea and air by law to law were made,
The vast design with living things was bade,
Urged in conception by a motive Power,
To forward roll to some predestined hour,
When evil triumphing no more, shall cease,
And brightly dawn the universal peace;
And from the ruin of a sinful world,
By righteous vengeance to destruction hurled,
Shall rise a new creation of the sky,
Our promised rest, the spirit home on high?
Why, why this change, O why must all,
That now is lovely in destruction fall,
And why should man be born to die,
Placed in the lonely tomb and rotting lie?
How could Sin enter the abode of bliss,
How rose Rebellion?   Where the vast abyss?
And Sin, base Sin, a blot still stands,
On all the beauty of the fairest lands,
And everything that man would cherish,
Is quickly blighted, soon must perish,
E'en the immortal soul would share,
The doom, the toil and desolate despair,

Of evil knowing no redress, perpetual night,

In endless absence from Eternal Light,

Had not Emmanuel come, free-willed, to die,

And by His guiltless blood a means supply,

That blackest sins might be forgiven,

And erring man attain to Heaven.

What pleasure can Imagination give,

When thinking of the day we learn't to live;

The night that saw the moving star,

O'er Bethlehem pause, gleam bright afar ?

Oh ! lonely beacon in the midnight skies,

In that dark time, to thee we lift our eyes,

. A weary world looks upward for relief,

From gloom, and wide distress and grief,

A weary world is waiting for the sign,

That now appears the king of David's line.

Hark ! hark ! Celestial anthems roll along,

Swells out on high the gathering seraph's song,

Bright Angels fill the vast profound,

And echo heaven's recording sound,

Which tells the World as breaks the morn,

That humbly, lowly, in a manger born,

Calm sleeps the babe, who shall forever save,

Mankind from ruin's yawning grave.

Oh ! Lonely beacon, oh ! Thou guiding light,

Still, still to thee, we raise our aching sight,

Bright emblem o'er a land of woe,

To bid each heart with hopes of glory glow,

And beckon nations lapsed from purity,

To upward gaze and grasp Eternity.

O happy, happy stars, that gave the Earth,

Their mildest light upon the Saviour's birth.

Did full-orbed Luna rise in cloudless space,

And did our beaming Planet swifter trace,

Her destined way throughout the glowing sky,

And all the spheres their music pour on high ;

Are these vast systems which we nightly see,

The same that hid their fire when on the tree,

The cursèd Cross, His stainless body hung,

And terror from the murderers wrung,

A knowledge of their heinous guilt,

The innocent blood base passion spilt ?

       *   *   *   *

Who does not watch with wondering eyes,

Soft gleaming Hesper o'er the gloaming rise,

Ere other stars can pierce that quiet light,

Which closely follows Sol's departing flight.
How swift along the darker Eastern skies,
That firm attendant on the pale moon flies,
A brilliant world around the Northern Pole,
Like some sweet angel, guardian of the soul?
Refulgent Hesper, thy mild beams illume
Sublime Imagination's power, as in the gloom
Of midnight seen, for Earth revolves with thee,
Along the starry sky, through Ether's boundless sea;
And all creation rolls, as fast as thou,
In strong attraction to the burning brow,
Of Him sole Monarch of terrestrial day,
In shining course, as ages pass away?
O power divine, how wondrous is thy law,
How stands the soul o'erwhelmed, lost in awe!
Here, here Imagination free can roam,
Unfettered, wander 'neath high Heaven's dome,
Loose wildest thought, regardless of the scope,
And learn the influence of balmiest Hope,
Till every sense the raptured moment feels,
And a delicious dream, from Spirit-realm steals.
O when the mind is held in lofty train,
And can for some brief space alone remain;

The soul forgets its clay-bound cells,

And wrapped in great conceptions dwells,

Which tell of Life, of Time without an end,

When both eternal, through the ages blend.

As o'er sweet features of an aged face,

Slow dawns the mild reflection of the grace,

Of Him whose likeness throughout life hath been,

Though not to mortal eye, yet clearly seen,

Engraved on heart and thoughts each hour,

And calms the terror of the unknown Power,

As earth's worn body fades away,

Swift hastening to lone regions of decay ;

So is it with the minds that constant keep,

When half mankind are held in sleep,

A long communion in the gliding years,

With the countless, ever-shining spheres.

What wonders burst on Galileo's eye,

When first with telescope he ranged the sky ;

How flew Imagination o'er his soul,

As far before him lay an ever-deepening goal ?

Rich and exhaustless, unsurveyed, unknown,

Save by some watcher of the plain, alone

At mid-night hour, or in the morning sleep,

As the "Great Bear" would down the heavens creep,
And meteors gleam with trailing light,
And bright "Orion" sink in Western flight.
Oh! when the Moon before his vision rolled,
And mountains, valleys, on her face unfold ;
When Venus, Jupiter, and Saturn, showed
Their glories, like dawn of sunlight glowed ;
And the celestial vault, as dust displayed,
A multitude of stars that never fade,
How rose in might and majesty arrayed,
Imagination's glorious form, sweet maid,
Attempered to a higher range of the sublime,
Sobered by thoughts of farthest springs of Time!
And these mould out a brow, expansive, grand,
Deep linèd with marks of self-command.
Imagination, then, on mighty pinion soars,
Beyond the starry worlds to distant shores,
Fed with increase of knowledge it can fly,
Past the wide boundaries of the naked eye,
Toward the bright spot where Paradise begins,
And every angel swiftly-entering brings,
Some storm-tossed spirit to the breast,
That longs to yield its everlasting rest.

Eternal Love and Joy, Eternal Peace, 'tis all
Our earth-born fancy here its own can call,
For none have told, none know, the bliss that waits,
The weary soul on passing Eden's gates.
It is a haven where some one has gone,
Worn out with toil, who for a period shone,
The meeting place, we shall united be,
And coffined faces once again will see.
They who have floated on the darksome tide,
The Stygian wave, where Fancy dares not glide,
A happy husband or an infant bright,
Who left fond arms for realms of light,
Whose gentle spirits drew themselves away,
And love, clasped naught but senseless clay,
Plunged on that lonely, flowing stream,
Where ray of sunshine cannot gleam,   [hand,
Swam to the farther bank, and grasped a shining
That bore them upward to the joyous land.
What is that place ?   Abode of gloom,
Where rank and fetid none can bloom ;
The thought of which destroys the smile,
Of youth and beauty free from guile,
To whose deep shade and night we go,

In perfect happiness or filled with woe !
Departed souls, ye of the envied blest,
Could ye return from your perpetual rest,
Give to the sons of men a passing glance,
In fleeting dream, or in the briefest trance,
At all the terrors they are doomed to brave,
To gain the glories held beyond the grave ;
I do not think that we would fear to die,
Nor dread within the tomb to calmly lie.
From earliest iufancy it is the banc,
That follows the awakening brain ;
The growing child is in the nursery told,
Of ghostly visions when the year is old,
Of hell-cats riding on the stormy wind,
Till deep within the trusting, wondering mind,
The timid fancy swiftly shapes such things,
That his own shadow, terror brings,
And tightly tucked amid the little cot,
Through sleepless nights upbraids his lot,
And asks himself the useless question, why,
If he were born, he must at some day die ?
Or when stern Sorrow's form has entered in,
And one he loves, pays out the penalty of sin,
Such tales are whispered round the room,

As evening throws its darkening gloom,
Of dogs that howled throughout the night,
And forms enveloped in a bluish light,
That mounted up the creaking stairs,
Their haggard features stamped with cares;
That when the stiffening limbs are laid,
In cold corruption's settled shade,
And pallid face enwrapped with horrid shroud,
His awe-struck heart beats strongly loud,
And o'er each sense quick memory prints,
The scenes of woe in dark, unfading tints;
While parents have improved the hour,
By telling of Death's relentless power;
And so he grows to manhood's years,
With recognised, but yet with unsolved fears,
Though youthful strength, may rob the blow
Of half its weight, and check the ardent flow
Of rushing thought, which comes on days,
When mind in higher flight delighted strays.
Thus, all enquiry into Death, the state
Of Future Life, and changeless fate,
Is left unanswered, treated silently,
Till older time arrives, of his maturity;

While woman, not in man's mad race,
Has naught to wipe away the early trace ;
And so the bloom of health will pale,
And breath will also sometimes fail,
And to herself must frequent weep,
When thinking of the grave's last sleep ;
Or if discourse in sweetest accents prove,
How Death has been, a great necessity of Love,
She dreads to hear what one would say,
Upon this worthless, suffering clay,
On the last effort and the lingering toil,
Before 'tis hidden underneath the soil.
Religion, firm Religion, thou alone,
Canst fill the heart with music's softest tone ;
Caught from celestial choirs beyond the sky,
And teach mankind unfearingly to die.
Oppression, Persecution, cannot tame,
Thy free-born spirit, a brighter flame
Will burn within the heart, and in the mind,
Where Tyranny is powerless to bind ;
For there thou singest to Imagination's ear,
And in thy song eternal joys appear,
And Reason broadens, as from distant gleams,

C

Flashes thy truth, through miracles and dreams.*

O I would not, with heedless manner, treat

The change, which ere the soul can meet,

Its great Creator spotless in the skies,

And to immortal glories step by step arise,

Must undergo to safely purge away,

The taint of sin which clings around decay.

For 'tis in truth an awful moment then,

And shrinks the hearts of strongest men,

When waning breath comes with the heavy eye,

And clammy dews about the forehead lie ;

When heaves the last convulsive throb,

And stands the being face to face with God.

Departed spirits, ye, I think, would say,

Fear not the stroke when low we lay,

When latest second has been numbered here,

Nor shed o'er transient Earth a silent tear !

For pain and anguish can distress no more,

They live not where the soul will soar,

And where our loved ones have in gladness gone,

We cannot dread to follow bravely on ;

---

* Not that Religion is now assisted in the slightest degree by mani-
festations of the supernatural, but that wherever this appears in
Holy Writ, its ethical tendency gives it the same value as ever.

Death is not what the mind conceived,

Or childish fancies had too oft believed ;

The weary body seeks, and welcomes sleep,

Does new-born life and fresher vigour reap,

To brightly hail the morn's returning gleam,

From slumber undisturbed by dream.

And so the soul along the course of time,

Desires to know again the heavenly clime,

Is worn and tried, is restless waiting here,

For recollection* brings from far a lovelier sphere,

When once it can this clay-house leave,

Where angel hosts in joy receive,

With triumph songs, God's sacred breath,

Victor o'er sin, the conqueror of Death.

Imagination ceases not, but hope appears

To free the heart from trace of parting fears,

And lead the sanguine mind to other lands,

Where some dear friend upon the boundary stands.

The struggling thief on Calvary's lone hill

---

* " Our life is but a sleep and a forgetting.
  The soul that rises with us our life's star,
  Hath elsewhere its setting and cometh from afar,
  Not in entire forgetfulness, and not in utter nakedness,
  But trailing clouds of glory do we come,
  From God who is our home."—*Wordsworth.*

Forgot the past, the present pain and ill,
When told that he with Christ would be,
That day in Paradise, and glory see.
Whose fancy could not sweep away,
Beyond the passing troubles of decay,
To dwell on Heaven's eternal peace,
Forever gained when care should cease ;
And who can fear to leave a changeful life,
To meet again a husband or a wife ?

V.

When sweet reflection captive holds the mind,
And filled with secret joy we slowly find
Too well-remembered spots our lonely way,
Now rise the scenes of many a bygone day !
This is the place where wisdom held her sway,
And this the field where passed the hours of play ;
Here flows the river still, whose cooling wave,
Did oft our youthful limbs with eddying ripples lave,
Behold the country, loved and known so well,
Its forest trees and silent paths, its bog or fell ;
All, all is there, but faces of the past are not,
Though forms that memory had well-nigh forgot,
Are fast recalled by each familiar scene ;

A gate, a style, a something that had been
Once pregnant with events of boyish days,
Speaks to the mind, to fancy's loving gaze.
Then, as we linger on the track of Time,
Fast hastening onward to an unknown clime,
Slowly arise the cherished thoughts of life,
Born in a moment 'mid the toil and strife ;
Born from the hope encircling early years,
Struggling to light and triumphing o'er fears.
Oh ! Memory where art thou now ? behold !
Dear Fancy joyfully her treasured stores unfold,
Call back again the vanished hours and days,
And pour o'er fond delights thy tributary praise.
Swift from recesses deep within the brain,
Imagination rises to their charmèd strain ;
Caught from the confines of the spirit's home,
Wild as the turmoil of the salt sea's foam,
Herself immortal, whispering songs that tell,
Of things unseen, where souls eternal dwell.
Soon every thought distinct creation takes,
Each form the higher Power combines, and shapes
The whole in orderly array, which passes by
Unknown to outward sight, before the inward eye.
Oh, happy hour ! Oh, day of earth-bred joy !

No holy pleasures can Imagination cloy ;
Pure as the streams which sparkling flowed,
Through the bright valleys of man's first abode ;
We lift our eyes, and all the world reveals
A softer beauty, while contentment steals
In peaceful way around the joyous heart,
And bids perplexing care, and toil, and woe depart.
We further gaze where shine ideal lights,
Which luminate mankind to those far flights
Of glorious Reason, ever longing to regain
The heritage once lost, which shall be theirs again ;
Till o'er the mind a true excitement spreads,
Wakes up each faculty, and gently threads,
A pleasing, unobstructed course along,
With brilliant vision and to sweetest song.
The dreams of youth, the plans of early years,
Formed when the phantom of ambition rears,
A mock-heroic life, and every pitfall screens,
Rise swiftly up, in wild enchanted scenes.
Yet, who would lose remembrance of the hour,
When first was felt that force of latent power,
Which opened wide the channels of desire,
And freer thoughts to highest deeds aspire.
Still onward, quickly onward, Imagination flies,

Gilding with hope all manhood's enterprise;
Ardent to win the foremost place of fame,
And dying to transmit an honourable name;
A newer courage dawns upon the soul,
Of high resolve, to gain the wished for goal,
To face Life's conflict, work its problem out,
Till Perseverance triumphs o'er unsettling Doubt.
Here, restless Fancy pictures to the eye,
A thousand shapes that fleetingly pass by;
Some are combined in scattered trains of thought,
And some half-formed in wanton pleasure caught;
Imagination, flows no more in forward wave,
But gentler now, as ocean's billows lave,
The yellow sands on some sequestered shore,
While far without the waters hoarsely roar;
Her tide is ebbing back, beyond the line,
Which separates the human part and the divine,
But leaves its trace upon the gladdened mind,
In calm repose and duty's laws defined.
The sun fast sinks beneath the western sky,
The song-birds cease their notes, and homeward fly;
All nature robes herself in sombre hue,
And love, and life, and light, depart from view.
Who is not moved when nature's charms unfold,

And deck the west in crimson and in gold,

When hill and dale grow tremulous with light,

And far-off waters daze the lingering sight?

When mighty clouds like mountain ranges rise,

In peaks and valleys float along the skies,

Hoary as age, bright with the brilliant glow

Of sunshine, white as the tints of the alpine snow.

Eternal Beauty!　Thou whose spirit sways

The soul of man with unexpressive praise,

And fillest all things from the humble flower,

To nature's hidden harmony, with universal power;

Thou who dost dwell, impenetrably grand,

On all that springs beneath Jehovah's hand,

Pregnant with knowledge of a higher state,

Beyond the present, and above dry rules of fate;

Speak to my heart, awake responsive beats,

And yield a glimpse within thy secret seats,

Oh, tell what forms more varied in detail,

In climes divine, lie far behind thy veil;

Say, if this earthly loveliness was born,

As God's bright signet, on creation's morn,

For thou dost bloom to Reason's sight unknown,

Thy mystic glory lives for Heaven alone,

But raises man to pierce through dull despair,

And freely breathe amid empyrean air;
To tread the path by ancient martyrs trod,
And feel, however slight, in contact with his God.
Eternal Beauty ! Still thy stamp we trace,
Through long descent upon the human race,
Sprung from a lineage high and purest birth,
Though ruled by passions, fettered to the Earth;
Still can each sense perceive thy subtle spell,
Like Ocean murmuring round a curvèd shell,
In gentle winds amid some lonely Pine,
Or Music's distant notes of melody divine;
In Spring's bright garment of refreshing green,
In smiling Peace o'er Summer's sweetest scene,
From all the fragrance of the blooming rose,
That over Eastern climes the Zephyr blows.
Oh ! who has heard from corn-field slowly rise,
The matchless carol, glory of the skies,
Nor felt unmoved, nor knew a current flow,
Of tender sympathy in heightening glow.
Celestial Bird ! I hear thy beauteous note,
From Heaven's blue vault upon my spirit float;
Though all in fancy, yet I hear thee still,
Most beautiful, where lie in chambers chill,
The lonely dead, the Stranger's silent home;

But thou around them dost in freedom roam,
And every eve above each grass-grown grave,
As if from Lethe's stream their souls to save,
Pour forth in praise, melodiously and long,
Thy glorious, thy heaven-aspiring song.
O happy Bird! O ever-mounting Lark!
Thy song flows sweetest o'er the Isle of Sark,
No wanton change disturbs the peaceful land,
With wildest craze of innovating hand,
Girt by the sea, whose foaming waters break,
Along the rocky shore, and silent caverns wake.
Thrice happy Bird! Thy song of love doth sway
The human heart when youth has passed away;
Thy music speaks to Fancy's agèd ear,
And scenes arise of many a vanished year,
Dear scenes of love, when mutual passion grew,
'Mid tender vows, strong-pledged and true.
Delight of Age, to linger o'er the place,
Once thought a heaven, hallowed by a face;
To call again, from depths in memory stored,
The burning love that erst thy ardour poured;
To see through Fancy's sight the trembling maid,
Whose throbbing bosom caused each word to fade,
Those accents which the heart in mad desire,

Hoped then to learn as portion of the fire,
Which every feeling long suppressed consumes,
But joined to living love eternally illumes;
At last they came, but faltering first they come,
When all the being for a time was dumb,
Till both thy arms encircled close the form,
And panting breath was heavy, fast and warm.
Away, away, there is no perfect love,
Nor sweet Nirvana, save in realms above ;
But happiest hours beside a murmuring stream,
With flowing thought from Fancy's lofty dream,
When yon bright sun is hid behind the trees,
And softly steals along the evening breeze ;
Then great contentment spreads a gentle glow,
And absent voices speak in whispers low,
From other climes beyond the swelling sea,
From distant border-land of great eternity.
Oh, charm of charms, that castle-building gift,
Deep down the cells of memory to sift,
And draw the knowledge throughout life acquired,
Till with a seer's eye seem half inspired—
As when an antiquary, 'mid some ruin stands,
Of vanished might in far historic lands,
And views with outward eyes the mouldering stone

Feels all the solitude and joy to think alone,
His inward light repeoples the domain,
And forms of ages past come back again,
Imagination follows in a swifter course,
When visions of the years rise up from hidden source,
Pass in completeness o'er the lonely scenes,
And call to busy life, dead Kings and Queens ;
A Patriot's deeds, urged by the minstrel's song,
A nation's history, in adjusting wrong—
The strife for rights—such is the curious tale,
Long handed down aud told without avail ;
A grateful people raise in fatal hour,
Some Saviour of their race to highest power ;
And he, forgetful of the country's fame,
Sweeps on the land to aggrandize his name,
By slow degrees their freedom steals away,
Till liberty is licensed 'neath the Despot's sway.
Another ruler reigns, of generous parts,
Who fosters commerce and the liberal arts,
Redresses evil, learns the people's cares,
And health and happiness in proportion shares.
Time moves along and many rulers rise,
The tyranny of wealth saps highest enterprise,
Fierce competition bars the path of life,

And dampens energy on the eve of strife ;
Thought turns away to lands beyond the sea,
Where man and man live in equality,
To build a home in wilderness unknown,
And dwell in peace, untrammeled and alone.
Imagination forms ideal dreams of rest,
Of wealth acquired within the glowing west ;
Friend after friend departs from native shores,
Till one great tide of emigration pours,
Onward and onward to the newer clime,
But bearing ever on, the added wrecks of Time.
Thus has it been, Imagination leads
The human race, and animates their deeds,
Since that first hour on Shinar's lonely plain,
A tiny band, a remnant from the slain,
Since that sad day the great barbarian horde, [sword,
Through Europe swept, with fire-brand and with
To later times when starving thousands fled,
From ancient homes, the stranger's soil to tread.
Thus has it been—we still repeat to-day,
The lesson learnt from generations passed away ;
Immortal Greece, forerunner of our own
Great English empire and illustrious throne,
Forever firmly built on Democratic laws,

And ever safe while in the righteous cause ;

Great colonizing land, to thee we turn, [learn,

And in thy growth and death the fate of nations

Trace all the progress of Imagination's power,

And hail with joy thy Resurrection hour.

Oh tell me, what delirious moments rise,

When Athens shines upon the traveller's eyes ;

The home of art, the nursery of the world,

Till deep in ruin were her children hurled ;

Which if once seen, the haughty Roman knew,

'Twas useless toil to seek for further view,

Another clime beyond the deep blue sea,

As there was gathered all that then could be.

These are the hills, the mountains and the coasts,

Which saw the Medo-Persian's mighty hosts,

They too, beheld the conqueror of that day,

In his lone ship, an exile, sail away ;

Here Aristides dwelt, and free from lust,

Obtained the glorious title of " the Just ; "

And here the Macedonian king with specious right,

Urged Xerxes, claims, before Platæa's fight ;

Oh Pericles, thy name is printed on the land,

Thy fame survives man's oft-destroying hand ;

A sister State the fatal blow first gave,

When Sparta's galleys swept Egina's wave,
Which from the Hellespont victorious came,
And proud Lysander earned a doubtful fame.
Yet in thy sorrow one bright spot appears,
For mighty wisdom o'er the ruin rears
Her majesty sublime, a living light,
Great Socrates dispels the pagan night.
Ecstatic joy, to view that sacred soil,
Where "Athens wisest" lived in daily toil,
To breathe the air his poisoned bosom drew,
As stiffening death in gradual torpor grew ;
To know the clime where rival schools of Thought,
To plant humanity in mortals sought,
Where Epicurus, Plato, Aristotle taught,
And each the germs of greater knowledge caught;
Where rose Thalia and the Tragic Muse,
The lyric art, the verse of love's most varied hues.
Here was the home, the cradle of a race,
Who sprang to glory, died, but left their trace
Upon that time, to each succeeding age,
In science, art, and the ne'er dying page,
When Rome was steeped in deep barbarian gloom,
And her Augustan reign had yet to bloom.

Eternal Greece.   In Europe's darkest hour,
Thy language proved a renovating power,
Unlocked the secrets of the Christian creed,
And fed Imagination in her direst need;
O'er every mind the newer learning spread,
A newer life was breathed in nations dead,
And golden dreams arose of tranquil peace,
As wars and slaughter should forever cease;
But progress seeks not quiet and repose,
In toil and tumult, in the deadly throes
Of warring peoples, she must force a way,
To higher destiny, to brighter day.
Then England felt the change, the rush of life,
Threw off old forms and fiercer urged the strife,
A free religion swayed the human heart,
And gave strong impulse to new turns of art;
A purer prose, a greater burst of song,
Swept in full course, in mighty wave along;
The daring mariner in search of gain,
'Gainst every force sailed down the Spanish main;
Or bolder yet, in all the energy of soul,
Essayed to reach, the far, mysterious Pole;
And still the influence exists, imparted then,

Has moulded through the years a nobler race of men.
Such are the joys that contemplation gives,
Life is worth having, if man ever lives,
- To glean the knowledge which the earth displays,
O'er all her surface to his keenest gaze ;
Arrange it well within the corners of the brain,
Then come Imagination with thy glorious train
Of rushing thoughts, which ne'er can pale ;
Like nymphs and dryads of a wondrous tale,
Bright deities unknown, save through a guess,
As fancy places them in gorgeous dress ;
Envelop all our faculties at last,
And call some hero from the glimmering past,
Some mighty Poet of primeval race,
One glimpse allow, O draw us face to face,
That we who dwell upon their vast designs,
And freely worship them as living signs,
Of the great power that worked upon mankind,
In earliest stages of the human mind,
May see the forms that still yield us delight,
Though buried long ago from mortal sight.
For who reviewing lofty deeds of men,
That nearer raise our natures unto Heaven,

D

Can fail to wish his eyes could meet with those,
That must have glowed as the conceptions rose,
The thought will come, though Death to darkness
Oblivion has no power above their tombs.   [dooms,

.

VI.

Who has not sat entranced 'neath Music's spell,
Whose pulse doth not the wild vibrations tell,
When some lone strain hath caught the ear,
And starts from secret wells the silent tear ;
Who has not felt how music can impart,
A newer vigour to the care-worn heart,
Weary with fighting 'gainst life's swiftest stream,
And hope fast dwindling to a flickering gleam ?
Who does not know the feelings that arise,
And nerve the man to deeds of enterprise,
Teach him to grasp again with greater power,
The high ideal formed in earliest hour,
As every chord by master-spirit wrought,
Excites and elevates each hidden thought,
Bears the freed soul in ecstasy of flight,
To native sources of immortal light ?
O is there not some weird, forgotten lake,

Where no rude sounds the happy calm awake,
That mountains high surround on every side,
And blooming summers through the years abide ;
Where lonely isles in dark seclusion lie,
With ruined temples of an age gone by,
Whose ancient walls once heard in accents long,
The deep *Te Deum* rise, the sacred song,
When faith was pure as mind of youngest child,
Ere doctrines false religion had defiled ;
And where to keep remembrance of them still,
The saddest requiems the night air fill,
Heard only by the Poets of the land,
For they alone their charm could understand,
Whene'er the full-orbed Moon comes high in sight,
Far o'er the mountains beams a silvery light,
Casting long shadows down the rippling wave,
Stirred by soft winds the pebbly shore to lave ;
That in this quiet hour when Nature slept,
Forth from their homes the Genii crept,
Bright 'gainst the foliage of sombre green,
In lofty barge propelled by hands unseen,
While flows the dirge, as on Æolian strings,
And solemn visions to the fancy brings.

Such dreams as rise, when all alone,
One hears the night-wind's fitful moan,
Through some tall elm, and the lingering sigh,
Like troubled souls breathe out, when Death is nigh.
Eternal Music! In thy strains divine,
New lights of glory on the spirit shine,
Which upward moves from earthy bondage free,
And floats in rapture towards eternity;
Then, vague impressions on the feelings play,
Like twinkling stars o'er ocean's watery way,
Opening fresh thoughts of things unknown,
And filling language with a richer tone,*
Till man to man more sympathy displays,
And his deep heart re-echoes willing praise;
Then too, the mind exults in wider flight,
Through Reason's bounds, nor dreads the height,
Where Wisdom sits enthroned in lofty sway,
And all the nations glorious homage pay.
Eternal music! When the world is drear,
Thou art a Refuge from consuming fear,
Canst bear the weary o'er an adverse wave,
Which else had rolled above a silent grave;

* Herbert Spencer.

Thy strain doth lull the chafing heart to rest,
And fills with courage the dejected breast,
Bids hope arise with songs of earnest life,
And nerves the man to conquer in the strife.
As when an evil spirit over Israel's king,
Held high command, and nought could bring
Mild peace, or heal affliction's stroke,
Save the wild notes by master-hand awoke,
Forth came the youth anointed of the Lord,
To touch with magic art the harp's sweet chord,
Win back from chaos the dull-clouded brain,
And charm the warrior chief to life again;
Or when ill-fate o'er Scotland's queen did lower,
She nursed not woe within a lonely bower,
But rose supreme above her faithless friends,
And sought the power the Minstrel's passion lends,
Till ruthless steel the trusty Rizzio slew,
And tender love no more her bosom knew,
Risked all she had upon the battle's shock,
And took the path toward ruin and the block.
When heavy moods and blank despair appear,
And all the outlook of the future drear,
When love neglects to cheer the jaded heart,

And a cold world wears not the mask of art,
Naught else so quickly drives away regret,
The springing tears that both the eyelids wet,
When lingering long within the corners of the eye,
They do not flow, but yet they will not die,
As music's power when plaintive echoes roll,
And speaks its sadness to the inmost soul.
Then let the ear be soothed with songs divine,
" Songs without words " which bear immortal sign ;
O let " the Requiem's " solemn numbers flow,
Or great " Messiah," through the Hallelujah's glow ;
Or still, let some great Spirit be expressed,
And every thought with light of Fancy dressed,
As move the fingers o'er each trembling key,
And roam at will, Imagination free,
Moulding new harmonies, creating fast,
Fresh glorious melody of a distant past,
Where the eternal choirs glad anthems raise,
And hymn to God bright songs of praise,
Remembered by the soul, though undefined,
As earth-formed clogs relax upon the mind.
Beethoven, Mendelsohn and Handel, ye
Whose fame must live to dim eternity ;

Mozart, who died to fortune's smiles unknown,

Ere age had marked him lawfully his own,

A victim to the world's ungenerous hand,

In nameless grave within his native land;

Sublime Composers, how your strains will give,

To unformed nations that are yet to live,

Such wondrous joy, as now our hearts perceive,

When e'er thy notes seductive measures weave ;

But had we heard one of you touch the string

Of some sweet instrument, thy being fling,

With rapture in the soul-entrancing wave,

Which all the mind forgetful of the present gave,

How greater then had risen the delight ;

How wilder would have been Imagination's flight ;

Who having heard the Miserere's note,

In Sistine chapel o'er his senses float,

Who, having sat in some Cathedral aisle,

With massive pillars of the Norman style,

And heard from far the organ's mellow tones,

Fill with a thrilling life the silent stones,

As mount the echoes up the vast expanse,

And dreamy thoughts held the awed mind in trance,

Has failed to feel the power of Music's sway,

Or to the Heavenly Muse exalted tribute pay ?

VII.

He who has passed his days and nights in toil,
Has studied long and burnt the midnight oil,
Till bloodshot eyes the light of morning meet,
And shadeless, can no more the sunshine greet ;
Who slowly moves to the dread hour when all,
That now is seen, will strike each sightless ball,
A rolling orb, full-powerless to maintain,
With vigorous food, the ever busy brain,
May still rejoice, when Fancy gilds the mind,
And the lone heart though reason is resigned.
Who does not treat with reverence the blind,
They, who to fearful darkness are confined ;
Who, knowing Nature blooms around,
Must hear the spring-time's growing sound,
Who feel the sun's warm rays upon the cheek,
But cannot watch the shades of evening creep,
Along the darkening East, and change the West,
From glowing tints to sombre hues of rest ;
Who cannot tell as up the heavens climb,
The starry worlds throughout the lapse of time ;
Who listen to the river's rippling wave,
But do not see the banks its waters lave ;

Who live and move beneath some willing hand,
As babe or child does loving care demand ?
Oh, 'tis an awful thing the loss of sight,
To live a lifetime in perpetual night,   [gloom,
And wake from sleep each morning wrapped in
With knowledge that it is a changeless doom.
No more the eyes of her you love can shine,
With tender love, with ardour, caught from thine ;
No more thy soul can speak its fulness through,
The shattered orbs that hide it from all view,
Tell of the thoughts fast formed in cells behind,
And mirror the impressions of the mind.
When sweet contentment fills affliction's hours,
Like softest perfume of some cherished flowers,
And restless humour does not vanquish peace,
O'er life's pursuits which then must cease,
The highest joy the blind may all possess,
Can every thought array, in Fancy's dress.
The mind deprived of outward sight,
Illumes itself with bright, internal light,
And keener grows as contemplation yields,
The choicest food culled from its favourite fields ;
The man surveys, with power of inward eye,
Such scenes as deep in wildest nature lie ;

The cow-bell tinkling from a distant hill,
Or lamb's soft bleat, each thought will fill,
With tree, with shrub, with grass as green,
When o'er sweet Erin's pastures seen.
Haunts of brave youth recalls in vision clear,
As first to living eyes, and now to memory dear ;
Oft, yet recurs a prospect of the home,
Where childhood's footsteps learnt to roam,
And in succession pass well-counted friends,
Till every face some deep remembrance lends,
Forgotten things, forgotten sights come back,
Start up upon Imagination's track.
Still he enjoys the happy ties of life,
Far off removed from its immediate strife,
Can o'er the woes of other men lament,
And counsel patience and divine content ;
The well-known voice of wife will charm away,
All gloomy fears of premature decay,
Her step has grown familiar to the ear,
And forms of thought in various lights appear ;
His children's touch can to the mind reveal,
When o'er the body tiniest fingers steal,
How they progress through years of swift advance,
He too can feel each ardent loving glance,

Ere yet their powers, hard blindness understand,

And with their little hands clasped in his hand,

Take furtive glimpses at the bearded face,

And look again for recognition's trace.

Though sculptor's chisel, painter's brush,

Can ne'er call forth with glorious rush

Spontaneously, the tribute of a just applause,

Some noble work of living art the cause,

Yet literature will give a calm delight,

And pierce with gleams the shades of night.

In loving care, a chosen sister dear,

Throughout the days of every passing year,

May read the print his viewless eyes would see,

May feed the brain that else would empty be.

The Prince of Poets, Homer, he who lit the way,

For Greece advancing to a brilliant day,

Who told of Troy, Ulysses' wanderings long,

And wrought the structure of the epic song,

Felt in his later day the loneness of the blind,*

But unobscured lived the immortal mind ;

---

* With regard to the long-accepted tradition of Homer's blindness, but which during late years has been questioned, Gladstone
says, " what may be asserted with confidence is that Homer, if blind
at all, was only blind in later life."

Great Milton, struck with darkness, did not not shun,
To tell how Paradise was lost and won,
And who can say, when oft his spirit flew,
'Mong the creations which from fancy grew,
That he repined, or o'er his lot then grieved,
Or wished to be from black calamity relieved;
And He, who in a modern time, with aid
Of loving daughter, faithfully portrayed,
With matchless pen and more than magic art,
A charm his own, as if a picture to impart,
The sweet " Amenities of Literature," that joy
Unfailing, which ne'er the greatest votary will cloy,
Knew then the power of night's eternal gloom,
Knew all the sorrows of a settled doom.
Oh ! There are pleasures which the blind may feel,
Imagination's forms, their truest springs reveal,
From deep communions fearlessly can fly,
To dizzier heights, than boastful mortals try,
For naught of outward sight disturbs the eyes,
When mind on higher things desires to rise.

VIII.

How soon from middle-life we glide to age,
The earth's long journey done, the waiting stage,
Till comes our time to pass from toil and care,
To breathe a purer, fresher, more exalted air.
A few brief years must go in rapid change,
With varying history, wondrous strange,
The greatest sum of active life remains,
A trifling unit in the wide world's gains,
The tottering footstep and the old-worn face,
No more will move in the accustomed place;
A calm repose has settled on the brow,
Its wrinkled lines we trace not now;
The soft white hair clings to the forehead damp,
For light gleams not within the broken lamp.
When man to vigorous age prolonged has been,
And early friends have left life's scene;
When youthful people push the old away,
And newer thoughts the ancient paths array,
With progress ever pressing to a destined end,
The agèd by-laws of the world to mend,
Not re-arranged in Revolution's throes,

As mania of reform to madness grows,
But steadily and by degrees, improving forms,
That built up nations, weathering their storms,
Imagination may some pleasure give,
For he in other days, in other times can live;
His path of life in ordered courses runs,
And dismal toil, or dark ambition shuns,
He does not meet the breaking flush of day,
With surging thoughts that all the being sway,
But far in deep recesses of the heart,
From whence the springs of nature start,
Rise up eternal hopes of future joy,
Of calm content and peace without alloy.
The mind delights in retrospective view,
Of all that has been, and the faintest clue
Will follow through the numbered years,
That firmly leads where earliest scene appears.
There is a place, the harbour of the dead,
Where contemplations balmy influence shed,
And awe and sadness o'er the feelings creep,
That lost to life, such countless races sleep,
In narrow rows, at every head a stone,
Save those who died unwept for and unknown.

Here is the spot where age his friends may meet,

In fancy's sight their living spirits greet,

For those he loved are deep beneath the sod,

While their immortal parts are with their God;

Here they shall wake at the great Trumpet sound,

And burst in twain each grassy mound;

And sealed catacombs shall give to life,

The anxious mother and the long-lost wife.

A charm of age, to stand beside the grave,

Of some dear friend no mortal skill could save,

And think of days when life flowed in his frame,

And plans were formed to yield a future fame,

Before the steadfast eyes his features rise again,

His hand once more within thine own is lain,

His voice familiar sounds upon the ears,

And slowly starts the mist, producing tears;

Alas! too soon the vision fades away,

Amid the gleaming sunlight of the day,

An epitaph remains, to warn the passer by,

That he must wither, and prepare to die,   [breath,

And e'en the flowers which droop with autumn's

Tell their own tale and fall in lingering death.

When age is bending downward to the tomb,

Naught can the dying hour so well illume,
As when the mind may summon backward years,
And gaze at past events devoid of fears;
Imagination rises with a new delight,
Plumes her quick wings for farthest flight,
As death fast opens to the fleeting soul,
The never-ending pleasures of its goal;
Slow comes the music of the glad " well done,"
'Tis caught by him whose race is run,
Till, to the inner sight, and shining clear,
The well-known forms of wife and child appear,
Down, down they glide his Spirit to receive,
And then the body's breath takes its last heave,
Forth goes the Soul led to the halls above,
There to rejoice in one great life of love.

www.ingramcontent.com/pod-product-compliance
Lightning Source LLC
Chambersburg PA
CBHW022153020726
47496CB00008B/2696

*9 7 8 3 7 4 4 7 1 4 1 6 7 *